A Note to Parents

For many children, learning math is difficult and "I hate math!" is their first response — to which many parents silently add "Me, too!" Children often see adults comfortably reading and writing, but they rarely have such models for mathematics. And math fear can be catching!

The easy-to-read stories in this ***Hello Math*** series were written to give children a positive introduction to mathematics

an ... with a subject
th ... ***th*** stories make
m ... g, and fun for
ch ... he end of each
bo ... proach to help
ch ... nfidence.

E

• ... tory. The more
fa ... more they will
un

• ... "hear and see"
th

• ... played for fun.
Fo ... e activities that
en

• ... materials, help
ma

Le ... t math calls for
c ... nces that help
t ... symbols.

A ... math, other
id ... s, measuring,
co ... logically, and
th ... reading these
st ... will help your
ch ... ead of "I hate
m

...ucator
...hematics! Book

To Ruth Cohen

—J.R.

Library of Congress Cataloging-in-Publication Data

Rocklin, Joanne.
One hungry cat / by Joanne Rocklin; illustrated by Rowan Barnes-Murphy.
p. cm.—(Hello math reader. Level 3)
Summary: Tom the cat tries to evenly divide the snacks he has baked for himself and two friends, but after gobbling up a few treats, Tom is faced with a new division problem. Includes division activities.
ISBN 0-590-93972-6
[1. Division—Fiction. 2. Baking—Fiction. 3. Cats—Fiction.]
I. Barnes-Murphy, Rowan, ill. II. Title. III. Series.
PZ7.R59On 1997
[E]—dc20 96-23043
CIP
AC

12 11 10 9 8 7 6 5 4 3 2 1 7 8 9/9 0 1 2/0

Printed in the U.S.A. 24

First Scholastic printing, March 1997

One Hungry Cat

by Joanne Rocklin
Illustrated by Rowan Barnes-Murphy
Math Activities by Marilyn Burns

Hello Math Reader — Level 3

SCHOLASTIC INC.
New York Toronto London Auckland Sydney

Tom liked to bake yummy things.

One day Tom mixed
flour,
sugar,
water,
eggs,
butter,
and yummy chocolate
in a big bowl.

STIR, STIR!
WHIR, WHIR!

Tom baked one dozen chocolate cookies.

"I have enough yummy cookies
to share with my friends," he said.

Tom called Lulu.
Tom called Moe.

"Come to my house at
two o'clock for a party.
I have something yummy
to share!" said Tom.

Tom put three plates on the table.
He put the same number of
cookies on each plate.

“There!” said Tom.
“I like to be fair when I share.”

But Tom was hungry.
He could not wait until two o'clock.
He could not wait another minute!
Tom gobbled up the cookies
on his plate.
"Yummy!" said Tom.

Now Tom tried to put an equal
number of cookies on three plates.
He could not do it.

"Lulu and Moe will be mad
if I am not fair."
Tom gobbled up all the cookies
so Lulu and Moe would not be mad.

Tom looked at the clock.
"I still have enough time to bake
something yummy," he said.

Tom picked two lemons
from his lemon tree.

He mixed
flour,
sugar,
milk,
eggs,
butter,
and lemon juice in a bowl.

STIR, STIR!
WHIR, WHIR!

Tom baked a lemon cake.
The lemon cake was square.
"A square cake is easy to share,"
said Tom.

Tom cut the lemon cake in half.
"There are not enough pieces
to share," said Tom.

Tom cut the two pieces
in half again.
“Now there are too many pieces
to share,” Tom said.

So he ate one of the pieces.
“Yummy!” said Tom.

Tom put one piece of lemon cake
on each plate.
"There!" said Tom.
"I like to be fair when I share."

Tom sat down to wait
for Lulu and Moe.
SNIFF!
He smelled the yummy lemon cake.
CHOMP!

Tom ate half of one piece of cake.
He could not help it.

“Oh, no!” said Tom.
“I ate half of Lulu’s cake.
Now Lulu’s piece of cake is tiny.
Lulu will be sad.”

Tom did not want Lulu to be sad.
So Tom ate half of Moe’s cake, too.

Then Tom ate half of
his own piece of cake.

Now there was a tiny piece of lemon
cake on each plate.
"These pieces are too tiny
for a party," Tom said.
He gobbled up all the tiny
pieces of lemon cake.

Tom looked at the clock again.
Lulu and Moe would be coming
in half an hour.
"I *must* bake something yummy
for my friends!" said Tom.

Tom had a tiny bit of flour,
a tiny bit of sugar,
a tiny bit of milk,
and a tiny bit of butter.
He had one egg
and nine blueberries.

"That is not enough
to bake a dozen cookies.
That is not enough to bake a cake!
What will I do?" asked Tom.

Then Tom had a good idea.
He put everything into a little bowl.
"If I hurry, I can still bake
something yummy!" Tom said.

STIR!
WHIR!

Along came Lulu and Moe
at two o'clock.

"Here is something yummy
for you!" said Tom.
Tom gave one blueberry muffin
to Lulu.
He gave one blueberry muffin
to Moe.

"Tom, don't you want something yummy, too?" asked Lulu.
Tom patted his fat tummy.
He was not hungry.
"No," said Tom. "I baked the muffins just for the two of you."

"But that is not fair!" said Moe.
"We want to share with you!"

"I see blueberries in these muffins.
We will share our blueberries
with you!" said Lulu.
"Blueberries! Yummy!" said Tom.

Lulu and Moe counted
the blueberries.

"I have four blueberries
in my muffin," said Lulu.
"I have five blueberries
in my muffin," said Moe.

“Let’s see,” said Lulu.
“We will each give Tom two blueberries. That will be fair.”

“No, no!” said Moe.
“I will give Tom three blueberries. You will give Tom two blueberries.”

“No,” said Lulu. “I will give Tom one blueberry, and you—”

"STOP!" said Tom.
"Please do not give me anything.
It is all for you!"
"Tom!" said Lulu. "How nice of you!"
"You are a good friend," said Moe.
"Thank you," said Tom.

• About the Activities •

Before children formally study division in school, they have many informal experiences with two different types of division. Sometimes they share objects: "One for you, one for me, one for you, one for me," and then see how many each person gets. Other times they divide a number of objects into equal-size groups: "I need to glue three petals on each flower," and see how many paper flowers (i.e., groups) they can make. Both types of experience help children understand the importance of equal shares.

One Hungry Cat adds to your child's experience by presenting several situations that illustrate both types of division. Tom tries to divide cookies equally on the three plates. He tries to cut a cake into three equal parts. And Lulu and Moe try to share the blueberries equally among the three of them.

Activities, such as the ones that follow, not only support your child's learning about division, but also help develop number sense. The more chances children have to work with real-life numerical problems, the more opportunities they have to strengthen their understanding of numbers and their problem-solving ability. Be open to your child's interests, and have fun with math!

—Marilyn Burns

You'll find tips and suggestions for guiding the activities whenever you see a box like this!

Retelling the Story

Tom baked one dozen chocolate cookies. Do you know how many cookies there are in one dozen? If not, count the cookies shown in the story. (You should count 12.)

Tom put the same number of cookies on three plates. Use twelve pennies or buttons for cookies and share them among these three plates. You should have four "cookies" on each plate.

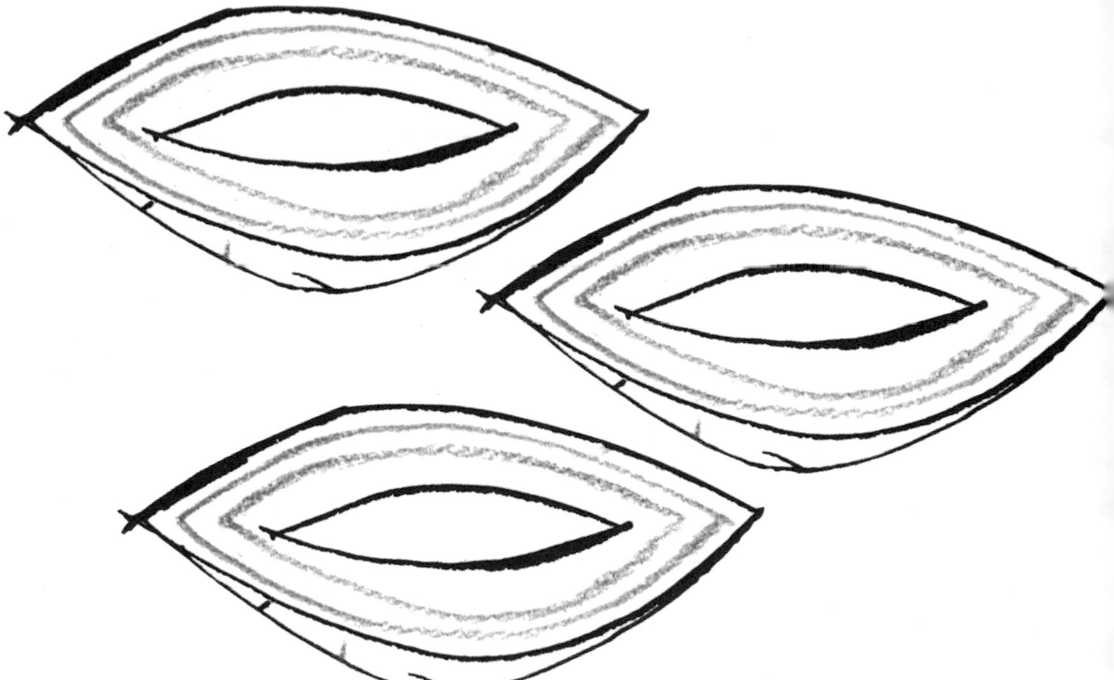

Before Lulu and Moe came, Tom ate all the cookies! Why did he do that?

Tom then baked a lemon cake and cut it into four pieces. What did he do with the pieces?

Cut a square cake out of paper and then cut it like Tom did — in half and half again. A hint: Folding first can help. Put a piece of your cake on each of the plates above.

Before Lulu and Moe came, Tom ate all the lemon cake! Why did he do that?

Then Tom baked two blueberry muffins, one for Lulu and one for Moe. Why didn't Tom bake a muffin for himself?

Lulu and Moe wanted to share their blueberries with Tom.

Lulu's muffin had four blueberries. Count out four pennies or buttons for blueberries and put them on Lulu's plate.

Moe's muffin had five blueberries. Count out five pennies or buttons and put them on Moe's plate.

Figure out how many blueberries Moe and Lulu would each have had to put on Tom's plate so they all had the same number.

Watching the Time

Tom invited Lulu and Moe to come at two o'clock for a snack. Is this a good time for a snack? Why or why not?

What are you usually doing at two o'clock? Do you do different things on weekends than during the week?

When Tom baked cookies, the cookies were ready long before two o'clock. Look at the clock in the picture that shows when Tom ate all of the cookies. Can you tell what time it was? How much more time was there before Lulu and Moe would come?

After Tom ate all the lemon cake, it was 1:30. How much more time was there before Lulu and Moe would arrive?

More About Sharing Cookies

After Tom baked a dozen cookies, he ate the four cookies on his plate. How many cookies were left? (You can use your pennies or buttons to figure this out.)

When Tom tried to share the eight cookies, he couldn't figure out how to give Lulu, Moe, and himself each the same amount. What was Tom's problem? Try sharing your pennies and see what happens.

What did Tom do?

Suppose you had six cookies. Could you share them equally on the three plates on page 36? Use six pennies or buttons to try this. Try other numbers of pennies or buttons and see which numbers you can share equally on three plates and which have leftovers.

Learning about sharing in equal groups helps prepare children for learning about division, with and without remainders.

A Different Lemon Cake

Some cakes are round. If Tom had baked a round lemon cake, how might he have cut it into three equal pieces? Cut a paper circle and see how you can divide it into three equal pieces.

It's typically difficult for children to see how to cut a circle into thirds. You might show your child how drawing a "Y" is a good way to approximate three equal parts. (A hint: start with a dot in the middle of the circle and have the three lines meet there.)

Blueberry Puzzles

Pretend that your pennies or buttons are blueberries and use the plates on page 36 to help you solve these blueberry puzzles.

Put two blueberries on Lulu's plate and four on Moe's plate. Figure out how to share them so Tom, Lulu, and Moe all have the same amount.

Try it again, starting with three blueberries on Lulu's plate and six on Moe's plate. Figure out how to share them so Tom, Lulu, and Moe all have the same amount.

Now you decide how many blueberries Lulu and Moe have to start. Be careful! Some problems are tricky and you will have leftovers! See which numbers leave leftovers and which numbers you can share without leftovers.

This activity basically poses the same problem for your child as "More About Sharing Cookies." However, the context is different and repeat experiences are valuable for understanding, as long as your child remains interested.